A Day at the Zoo

Grosset & Dunlap • New York

Cover: *bkgd*: David Messent/Photolibrary.com. *zebras*: Digital Vision/Getty Images. 1: *bkgd*: Rob Reichenfeld/DK Images. 3: *bkgd*: David Messent/Photolibrary.com. 5: *bkgd*: Rob Reichenfeld/DK Images. 6–7: *bkgd*: National Geographic/Getty Images. *monkeys*: Digital Vision/Getty Images. 8–9: *bkgd*: Margarette Mead/Getty Images/Image Bank. *parrots*: Digital Vision/Getty Images. 10–11: *bkgd*: Shahm Anup & Manoj/Animals Animals/Earth Scenes. *lions*: Digital Vision/Getty Images. 12–13: *bkgd*: Rob Reichenfeld/DK Images. *flamingos*: Ingo Jezierski/Taxi/Getty Images. 14–15 *bkgd*: National Geographic/Getty Images. *zebras*: Digital Vision/Getty Images. 16–17: *bkgd*: National Geographic/Getty Images. *bears*: National Geographic. 18–19: *bkgd*: PhotoDisc/Getty Images. *seals*: Digital Vision/Getty Images. 20–21: *bkgd*: Rob Reichenfeld/DK Images. *hippos*: Digital Vision/Getty Images. 22–23: *bkgd*: Comstock Images/Getty Images. *kangaroos*: Digital Vision/Getty Images. 24–25: *bkgd*: National Geographic/Getty Images. *elephants*: Digital Vision/Getty Images. 26–27: *bkgd*: Margarette Mead/Getty Images/Image Bank. *orangutans*: Akira Kaede/PhotoDisc/Getty Images. 28–29: *bkgd*: PhotoDisc/Getty Images. *penguin*: Eyewire collection/PhotoDisc/Getty Images. 30–31: *bkgd*: Shahm Anup & Manoj/Animals Animals/Earth Scenes. *giraffe with city backdrop*: Rob Reichenfeld/DK Images. *giraffes*: Digital Vision/Getty Images. 32: *bkgd*: Rob Reichenfeld/DK Images.

© 2004 The Wiggles Pty Ltd. U.S. Representative HIT Entertainment. All rights reserved. Published by Grosset & Dunlap, a division of Penguin Young Readers Group, 345 Hudson Street, New York, New York 10014. GROSSET & DUNLAP is a trademark of Penguin Group (USA) Inc. Printed in the U.S.A.

Library of Congress Cataloging-in-Publication Data

A day at the zoo.
    p. cm. — (The Wiggles)
  Summary: The Wiggles spend time together at the zoo enjoying the antics of the animals.
  ISBN 0-448-43601-9 (pbk.)
 [1. Zoos—Fiction. 2. Zoo animals—Fiction. 3. Stories in rhyme.] I. Series.
 PZ8.3.L549417 2004
 [E]—dc22
                            2003024924

ISBN 0-448-43601-9   10 9 8 7 6 5 4 3 2 1

A Day at the Zoo

Grosset & Dunlap

One day, we didn't know what to do.

We saw three funny monkeys chatting away.

We wished we knew what they were trying to say.

The parrots were perched high in a tree.

From way up there, what can they see?

The lions were next, a total of four.

The biggest one let out the loudest ROAR!

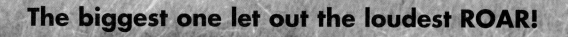

The flamingos stood two by two

with bright pink feathers in a lake so blue.

At the pond, the zebras took a long sip,

then went right in for a nice, cool dip.

The little bears were scampering around,

rolling and tumbling all over the ground.

We spotted two seals kissing each other—

a cute little baby and her mother.

Down in the water, the big hippos float.

"Ahoy there, me hearties, just like a boat!"

The kangaroos had a bite to eat.

A lunch of grass is a tasty treat!

Check out the elephants taking a bath.

They were so funny, we all had to laugh!

The baby orangutan will try anything.

She'll even use her mom for a swing!

That penguin looks like quite a nice fellow,

wearing a tuxedo with his hair that's so yellow.

No other animal is so tall or so grand

as the long-necked giraffe
who roams through the land.

We loved all the animals and hope you did, too. It's fun spending time with our friends at the zoo!